Houghton Mifflin Books for Children is an imprint of Houghton Mifflin Harcourt Publishing Company.

www.hmhbooks.com

Translation adapted by Jamie White

The text of this book is set in Adobe Garamond Pro.
The illustrations are watercolor and pencil.

Library of Congress Cataloging-in-Publication Data
Liu, Siyuan, 1964–
Gus, the dinosaur bus / written by Julia Liu ; illustrated by Bei Lynn.
p. cm.
Summary: Even though the school children think Gus the dinosaur bus is a great way to get
to school, his size is causing traffic problems for the principle and the town.

ISBN 978-0-547-90573-0

[1. Dinosaurs—Fiction. 2. School buses—Fiction. 3. Traffic congestion—Fiction.]
I. Lynn, Bei, ill. II. Title.
PZ7.L7394Gus 2013
[E]—dc23
2012018091

Manufactured in China
SCP 10 9 8 7 6 5 4 3 2 1
4500405488

Gus, the Dinosaur Bus

Written by Julia Liu
Illustrated by Bei Lynn

Houghton Mifflin Books for Children
Houghton Mifflin Harcourt
Boston   New York   2013

In the city, children are going to school.
Some walk.
Some ride in a car.
Some take a yellow bus.
But the lucky children of one school ride something different.

Gus, the dinosaur bus!

Every morning, Gus stomps down the streets to pick up his passengers. Nobody sleeps late or pretends to be sick. They can't wait for Gus to arrive.

Who needs a bus stop when you have a dinosaur bus? Gus comes right to the door. The children who live in apartments don't even need to walk downstairs. They hop out their windows and slide down to their seats.

Wheee!

Riding a dinosaur bus means never stopping for gas or being stuck in traffic.
"Honk! Honk! Dinosaur coming through!" the people shout.
Gus is careful not to step on any cars. But still, his big feet are a worry, so . . .

The city makes a new road just for Gus.
Along his route, people leave him snacks. Like two tons of french fries.
Road crews repair the dino-size potholes that Gus accidentally leaves behind.

Everyone at school loves Gus.
He helps them reach high places . . . and a supersaurus makes a good umbrella.

But life is not perfect for a dinosaur bus.

Gus is so tall that he often gets tangled in telephone lines.
He bumps his head on overpasses. He has been known to
knock down a traffic light or two.

When you're as wide as a tennis court, you can cause traffic jams for miles and miles. And it's not easy to cross bridges when you weigh as much as five elephants.

Careful, Gus!

Gus's tail is trouble too. Sometimes when he turns corners, he knocks down a house roof. Lately, the school is getting more and more complaints. Police officers keep dropping off tickets. The bills to fix the things Gus has broken are piling up.

"Gus is causing a BIG fuss!" says the principal. "What am I going to do?"

The principal has no choice. He pulls Gus off the road. Gus is so sad that he hides in the gym and cries and cries. Just one of Gus's tears could fill a bathtub. Each one falls to the ground with a

SPLAT!

The children crowd into the gym to cheer him up.

"Don't worry," they say, hugging their big green friend. "We will keep you company."

Gus is beginning to feel better. But — oh, no! The smallest girl has lost hold of his neck and is sliding down it.

"Whoa!" she cries . . .

"Hey!" she shouts. "Where did this pool come from?"
"Look, Gus!" says the teacher. "You've made a swimming pool with your tears."

The children cheer. "Hooray! Gus can play with us again!"
And they slide into their new pool.

Now Gus is no longer a dinosaur bus.
He's Gus, the dinosaur slide!
And swing.
And playground.

Every day, the children visit him to swim, slide, swing, and climb.
Maybe one day you can visit Gus too. But you'll have to be patient.

The line is long.